ENVY

Cherie Mitchell

Envy

By Cherie Mitchell

Published by The Little French eBooks

Art Cover by Ruth Cazaña Rojas

Copyright 2020- Cherie Mitchell

1

The ominous opening of the door at the end of the hall, this afternoon, should have warned her. If she was only a little faster, she would have been gone by now.

"Oh, you're still here, Mel. I thought you might be gone for the day. Can you do this for me, please?"

She looks at the sheath of papers her boss, Cary, hands her and sighs to herself. She smiles brightly at him. "No problem at all, Cary. Do you need these by tomorrow morning?" He does not arrive at work until around nine-thirty each morning and she starts at eight. If she begins the task as soon as she arrives, it will be completed and on his desk before he walks in.

Cary looks at his watch and shakes his head. "Sorry, Mel, I need it today. Tonight, actually. I have a dinner appointment with Reynolds and I need to present this to him. There are several aspects of the proposal I need him to sign off on before he flies to Auckland tomorrow. It won't be an issue, will it? Can you get it done?" His tone leaves no room for argument.

She nods, glancing at the time on her computer desktop. She will not be out of here before six and she is supposed to meet her boyfriend, Ben, at six-thirty. She opens Word and begins typing. "I'll bring it in as soon as it's complete." She does not look up from the keyboard, but out of the corner of her eye she sees him walk away. No thanks and no apology.

The door to his office closes as she keeps typing. This is happening far too often. She seldom takes lunch breaks and he wants her at work by eight each morning in order to take his calls before he arrives. If she stays until six, she is working ten hour days, which her salary certainly does not reflect. The position of Cary's Personal Assistant carries a certain amount of status and respect within the office, but no one really sees the true drudgery of the role.

She inserts a table onto the page and begins typing each point for discussion, leaving enough room for Cary to add notes. She does not take much notice of what she is typing. Her job involves a lot of copy typing and much of it is technical information and specifications. She has mastered the art of typing on auto pilot. It is a pity she cannot command a pilot's salary.

Andrea pokes her head around the door. She has her handbag over her shoulder and is wearing her *I'm out of here* expression. "Staying late again, Mel? It must be nice to be so essential to the business."

She makes a face at her and keeps on typing. Andrea knows the real facts of her position within the company, and she often gives her a hard time about it. She is not in the mood to hear any unwanted advice right now.

"See you tomorrow," Andrea calls as she opens the door leading out into the street. "I expect you'll still be at your desk when I get in." The door slams shut behind her.

"Very funny." She glances at the stack of papers piled beside her computer. She has barely made a dent in them. For a moment, she wants to get up, collect her bag, and run out the door after Andrea, leaving her work scattered where it lay. She continues typing.

At 6:05, she makes the final spell check correction before saving the file. She switches off the computer and picks up her handbag. Walking up the hallway, she knocks lightly on Cary's door. "The document is on your F Drive, Cary. Good luck with the meeting. See you tomorrow."

She hears him mutter something from behind the closed door and continues on her way. Her mind is already elsewhere. If she hurries, she should make it just in time to meet Ben for a quick dinner before they go to the movie. She glances at herself in the rear view mirror, as she falls into the driver's seat. She looks pale and frazzled, and her hair is limp and dull. There is no time for more than a quick ruffle of her hair and a slick of lip gloss. Ben will be waiting, impatiently, for her. He does not like to be kept waiting.

She drives to the mall where they are meeting. Tonight is late night shopping at The Palms and the car park is full. She crawls along the rows, hoping to spot an empty space. Glancing at the clock on the dashboard, it is already six-forty.

Finally, she finds a parking space at the far end of the car park. It is a good five-minute walk from the restaurant where Ben is waiting. She pictures him tapping his fingers on the table and looking repeatedly at his watch. She hurries toward the mall entrance, putting her head down against the weather. The clouds are darkening and it is raining. She is quickly soaked through, as she dashes through puddles to the entrance.

She and Ben have been dating for six months. As she tells her friends, their relationship is okay. It certainly is not fireworks and passion, but she prefers to be partnered rather than single, which sometimes leads to not choosing the best boyfriends. Ben is often snappy, critical of her appearance at the best of times, and he quickly grows impatient with her over any number of things. However, she clings desperately to the relationship, because she cannot bear the thought of being alone. To be alone would show the world she is unwanted and undesirable.

The heel of her shoe breaks just as she runs through the door of the restaurant, fifteen minutes late, dripping wet, tired, and on edge. She stumbles forward, throwing her hands out in an attempt to save herself as she hurtles toward the floor. Suddenly, she is caught by a pair of strong arms and pulled back onto her feet. She gasps in surprise while her heart pounds in her throat.

"Are you alright?"

She looks up into the hazel eyes of one of the most attractive men she has ever seen in her life. He has thick brown hair curling back from his face and deep smile lines on each side of his mouth. His skin is smooth and tanned, with just a hint of five o'clock shadow around the jawline. She noticess his hands are still on her arms. His touch is burning through the thin fabric of her top. She glances down, momentarily, and he lets go.

"Are you alright?" he asks, again.

"I'm fine, thank you," she stammers, her face flush with embarrassment. She bends down and picks up her broken heel, holding out the pieces to show her rescuer. "My shoe broke. I'm meeting my boyfriend." She begins gabbling. She looks around, hoping to spot Ben. She sees him at a leaner by the far wall and waves. He does not wave back. "Thank you, again," she says to the man. She hops, awkwardly, toward Ben, carrying her broken heel and feeling every pair of eyes in the bar on her.

"Hi, darling," she says brightly, placing her wet handbag and broken heel on the leaner table top. "Sorry I'm late." She can feel people watching her, their eyes boring into her back.

Ben stares at her, aghast. "My god, Mel. The entrance you made was so embarrassing. You threw yourself through the door and into that poor guy's arms. Look at you. You're a complete state, dripping wet, and no makeup. I've seen drowned rats looking better than you."

"Cary asked me to work late, it's raining outside, and my shoe broke," she says quietly, wishing he would lower his voice.

He sets his empty glass down on the table. "Mel, I don't think this is working. I don't think our relationship is working. I've felt this way for a while now, and that little incident in the doorway just confirmed it for me. I was going to talk to you over the weekend about this, but it's probably best we finish up now."

She stares at him. *What did he just say? Was it what she thought she heard? Surely not.* She struggles to get her thoughts straight. "What do you mean, Ben?"

He shakes his head, impatiently. "Mel, don't be so bloody dense. I'm not interested in continuing in a relationship with you and I think it's best if we finish up now." He stands up. "Have a nice life." He walks away without a backward glance.

She stares after him. *What just happened? Surely, she wasn't just dumped?*

She looks around, hoping no one has overhead. No one else is paying her the slightest bit of attention, anymore. She takes her coat off and signals to the waitress. Damn him, she is not going to run weeping out the door. She is having a glass of wine while she is here. It has been an awful day and she deserves a drink.

The waitress returns with her wine and places it in front of her.

"Thank you." She stares at the wood panel wall and considers her feelings. *Should she be feeling dismayed and heartbroken?* She has just been dumped on top of a very tiring day. She searches her mind for the slightest twinge of despair. She is surprised to find she feels a little relieved. It is draining keeping up with Ben's moods and always striving to make him happy, even though she knows she never can.

Pleased to discover she is not poised on the brink of a meltdown, she sits back and takes a sip of her wine. She'll order herself a bowl of chips with garlic aioli, as Ben is no longer around to complain about her garlic breath. And, dammit, she'll go to the movie by herself. She has been looking forward to seeing it. The evening suddenly appears to be a little brighter.

She drives home after the movie, still savouring the taste of the garlic aioli. The film was excellent, the rain stopped, her clothes are dry, and her earlier glass of wine left her feeling mellow. She thought back over the evening's events. Ben dumped her and she really does not care. *Are those feelings changing since she's had time to let it sink in? Does she suddenly care? Will she collapse in a sobbing heap as soon as she gets home?* She doubts it. Now that the relationship is over, she realizes how unsuitable it was. She also knows she would never have ended it herself.

She drives up her driveway and parks the car in the garage. Tomorrow is Friday, and then it will be the weekend and she does not have a boyfriend. She sits in her car for a few minutes, thinking. She has always had a boyfriend – when her relationships end she always picks up again with someone else, almost immediately. However, now that her relationship with Ben is over, she feels nothing but relief. *Maybe, for the first time in her life, she should spend some time alone?* Making choices for herself this evening has been a pleasant novelty. Still thinking, she walks up the pathway toward her house.

Cherie Mitchell

2

Friday passes quickly at work. Cary rings and says he will not be coming into the office until after eleven, stating that his meeting the night before ran very late. Andrea makes the most of his absence, perching herself on the edge of Mel's desk to hear her review of the movie, while sipping a cup of coffee from the newly installed café machine in the break room.

"I like the sound of it," Andrea muses. "I wonder if I can get Matty to come with me? But I think he's going 4-wheel driving this weekend with his mates. I'd like to go to the movie on my own. Indulgently order a chocolate ice cream and sit in the dark eating popcorn without him telling me I'll get fat." She looks dreamily into the distance, a small smile playing across her face.

"Oh, Ben broke up with me too," Mel says, while nonchalantly opening her desk drawer and taking out her notebook as if she just commented on the weather.

"What?" Andrea stares at her in surprise, her coffee cup poised in mid-air. "How are you? Are you ok, Mel? I thought you guys were doing well?"

She shrugs. "I feel fine. I'm a bit relieved, in a way. I was never going to be the one to finish it and the relationship wasn't going anywhere. No, we weren't doing well. We never had too much in common to begin with."

"Well, I guess if you're ok with it, that's all that matters." Andrea looks at her curiously, as if she is waiting for her to say something more.

Mel glances out the window as a black Mazda swings into the parking spot by the door. "Cary just pulled into the car park. You better go back to your desk and make yourself look busy."

Cary walks in shortly and comes straight across to her desk, balancing his briefcase and a stack of documents in his arms. "Mel," he says gravely with a serious face. "Give me five minutes to get myself settled, and then I'd like you to come in for a chat." He turns away without another word and walks into his office, closing the door firmly behind him.

She stares at her boss's closed door as an uneasy sensation rises up in the pit of her stomach. She shuffles things around her desk, unable to work while she fills in time. Carey never asks her to come in for a *chat*. She watches the clock tick slowly until ten minutes has passed before getting up and knocking on Cary's door. She takes a deep breath and smooths her skirt over her hips as she waits. She has a bad feeling about this.

"Come in," Cary calls, his tone heavy and abrupt.

She pushes open the door, her nervous hand nearly slipping off the handle, and walks into the office. Cary looks at her but does not say anything. He indicates with a wave of his hand she should take a seat in the chair in front of his desk. She sits down, nervously, and wipes her hands down her skirt. Cary's expansive office suddenly feels way too small, and she thinks of a hundred places she'd rather be.

He gazes at her, from the other side of his wide oak desk, for a long moment. His normally impassive face is solemn and drawn, which does nothing for her equilibrium. He clears his throat and shuffles the paperwork in front of him. "Mel, you have worked with me for quite some time now and I appreciate the hours you put into this job. However, the major part of the project that I'm currently working on needs to be completed in Sydney. There is no way around it. For the duration of the next stage of the project I will be based in the Sydney office. Reynolds and I shook on the deal over dinner last night. We expect that this stage of the project will last 18 months to two years, and that's erring on the side of caution." He glances down at his desk for several beats, as if preparing the right way to deliver his news, and then back at her. She is alarmed to see his expression is compassionate and sympathetic. She would prefer it if he looked cross or annoyed. Sympathy generally means bad news. She forces herself to concentrate on what he is saying.

"Therefore, as much as it pains me, I will no longer require your services as a PA. I will be employee-sharing with Reynolds whilst based in Sydney. Faye is the PA in the office over there. I'm sure you spoke to her on occasion. She is highly efficient and able to support the both of us. Mel, I'll get straight to the point. Unfortunately, what this means for you is a redundancy. You will be adequately compensated with a redundancy payout, of course, and you are welcome to go and consult with an HR professional if you feel that you need the support or further information as to where you stand. I'm sorry." He waits for her reaction.

She stares at him, struggling to make sense of what he said. This news is a complete bolt from the blue. Not in a million years has she ever imagined her job was not secure. *What will she do?* She has worked there for the past five years, and despite the fact she often complains about the work and knows she is not paid well for the hours she puts in, it is a steady income. She has no idea what the job market is like. *Where will she find another job? How can this be happening?*

"Mel?" Cary says gently, "I realize this is a shock to you. However, as I said, you will receive a very reasonable redundancy package. You're a smart girl, and I don't imagine you'll have a difficult time finding another job. Mel, I would like to thank you for the enormous help you have been over the past five years." He rises, effectively calling their meeting to a close.

Mel stands up, feeling disorientated and still not entirely sure what just happened.

Cary holds out his large hand to envelop her's and gives it a firm shake. "Thank you again, Mel, and I wish you the very best." He pulls open his desk drawer, takes out a large white envelope, and pushes it across the desk toward her. "You will find all the details of your redundancy package in here, along with a written reference from me. Of course, I will also be happy to act as a verbal reference. As I said, please consult with an HR professional if you think it is necessary, although I can assure you we have followed all the relevant industry standards and requirements. I understand this must be a shock to you. You can collect your things and go now, if you prefer. I don't expect you to finish out the day." His impassive expression falls away for a moment and she sees the concerned and kindly man behind his professionalism. He clears his throat and looks toward the door. Their discussion is over.

"Thank you." She turns and walks toward the door, holding her back rigid and placing her feet carefully in front of her so she does not stumble. *What is she thanking him for?* He just gave her the sack. Human etiquette can be so illogical at times.

She stands numbly in front of her desk. *Should she log out? Should she at least delete her personal emails from Outlook? What was the point? Cary was hardly going to fire her for sending and receiving a few personal emails since he already terminated her position. Besides, as he said, the company did everything by the book, which she does not doubt.* She picks up her bag and walks toward the door, making up her mind she does not want to see or speak to anyone. She just wants to get out of there. She will email Andrea later and update her, but she knows Cary will make some kind of announcement to the other staff.

She sits in her car for a moment, before starting the engine. It is 11.30. From this moment on she has no job. *Where should she go?* She is *always* at work at this time. The world she stares at through the windscreen seems different, slightly off centre and fuzzy around the edges. She knows she does not want to go home to sit alone in the quiet of her house. She pulls out of the car park and heads toward Dyers Pass Road. She will go to the Port Hills, the low slopes which overlook the city. They have always been her thinking place, her place to be still and sort through the things troubling her.

Cherie Mitchell

She takes the turn onto Victoria Park and parks in the lot. Mothers with children dawdle around the swings and slide, and walkers with day packs are setting off toward the many walking paths. She parks the car and climbs out. Taking the envelope from Cary with her, she veers away from the noisy playground. She walks toward the part of the hillside that looks over the plains, an area of scrubby bushes and knotty trees with a natural rocky outlook. The view is spectacular. Instagram-worthy in any weather. Today, she barely notices it.

She finds a patch of grass away from the parking lot and road, a pretty spot surrounded by native bush and tussock. From here, she can see the patchwork green of the plains and the shadowy blue of the alpine mountain range, far off in the distance. She sits for a while, allowing the green and the blue and the peace to wash over her. A bird calls from a nearby tree, its happy musical tone piercing the air. A light breeze lifts strands of Mel's hair and the sun warms her face. It would be perfect any other day, but today is not just any other day. Today is the day she lost her job.

She sighs and finally opens the envelope to discover her net worth in the eyes of the company. She reads the reference from Cary first. It is very good, excellent in fact, and she is grateful for that. She checks the attached payslip. As well as her current week's wages and her due leave days (now paid out, according to the typewritten note), they gave her approximately three months wages as a redundancy payment. *Surely, she will find another position before the money runs out?* She thinks fleetingly of Ben. If he knew of this latest change in circumstances he would tell her it is not enough money and she should fight the redundancy. But Ben's opinion is no longer her concern and she is happy enough with the settlement. Perhaps, it is time for a change, anyway – she is overworked and underpaid for the effort she is putting in. She stands up and brushes the dust off the back of her skirt. There is nothing else to do but go home and get on with the rest of her life. Everything has been irreversibly altered in the past 24 hours, and she has no idea what now lies ahead. There is no point in moping about it.

3

Mel rings her sister, Jessie, the next morning and arranges to meet her for a coffee.

"What's up? What's been happening?" Jessie asks curiously. "You sound different. Are you ok?"

She hesitates before answering, imagining her sister with her pretty eyes narrowing and her ears pricked for any sign of disaster, and decides it will be best to deliver her news in person. "I'm fine. Just a little tired. See you at two, Jess."

She putters around the house all morning, not really doing much at all, except mulling over her newly unemployed and newly single statuses. The loss of Ben does not seem to have much of an impact yet, but she supposes the fact she is single will hit her soon enough. She is not fond of being on her own, and it is a state she generally tries to avoid. It will not be until Monday morning, with no job to go to, that her lack of work will become a reality.

She meets Jessie at the Coffee Co-Op, a big barn coffee shop with a relaxed atmosphere, wide wooden rafters, cheerful paintings, plenty of comfortable tables and chairs, and slouchy sofas on which to pass the time of day. The staff are young and friendly, and their famous Jail breaker coffee is superb. She is also particularly fond of their blackberry slice, a homemade fruity, biscuity treat. Her mouth begins to water.

She walks into the coffee shop and is immediately hit with the low hum of chatter and laughter. The cafe is busy as usual, with its mixed clientele of cool young things, mothers escaping for a Saturday afternoon gossip session with their friends while their husbands play house dad, and a bunch of older people looking pleased and smug they'd found such a comfortable and accessible coffee spot in their local area. Looking around for Jessie, she sees her walking in the door with a broad grin on her face.

"Mel!" Jessie swoops in, enveloping her in one of her warm hugs.

She hugs her back, already feeling lighter just from being in her sister's presence. "Coffee? A cappuccino and a cake? I'll get it. You go and find us a table." She stands in the queue for a few minutes and places their order. She is disappointed to find the blackberry slice is sold out, and orders a piece of chocolate cake and a napoleon cream instead. The food is great, and the serving sizes more than ample. She takes the table number from the youth behind the counter and goes to join Jess at one of the dark-stained wooden tables.

"So?" Jessie asks as she brushes a few stray crumbs off the table top, instantly falling into mommy-mode. "Tell me your news."

She takes a deep breath. "I got dumped and fired. In that order. In less than 24 hours. How about you? What have you been up to lately?" She bares her teeth into a false smile, which she knows her sister will see right through.

"What?" Jessie shrieks. She looks around the café, apologetically, and lowers her voice. "Ok, I'm not too surprised about the Ben breakup as it was blatantly clear that you two weren't the perfect match. But your *job*? You've been there forever. How did that happen? Why?"

The waitress arrives at their table with their order and places the overflowing plates in front of the girls. "Enjoy."

"Napoleon cream or chocolate cake? Or half each?" She is already cutting the cakes in half with her fork. She places two pieces on each plate and passes one plate to Jessie, who has been staring at her with her mouth wide open ever since she made her announcement.

"Mel, you lost your job? And yet, you hardly seem concerned. I don't understand."

She pops a forkful of napoleon cream into her mouth and half-shuts her eyes in satisfaction. She nods as she mumbles through the mouthful of cake. "Yes, I got fired."

"Mel, for God's sake, stop stuffing that cake into your face and talk to me. It's not as if you're starving to death. You've got more than enough spare pounds to keep you sustained and away from the edge of starvation." Jess is blunt, as only a sister can be. "How did you lose your job?"

She swallows her mouthful of food and reluctantly puts her fork down. She explains to Jessie how Cary called her into his office and passed her the dreaded white envelope, along with her redundancy payout.

Jessie shakes her head. "I think it is very rude of the company to let you go like that. How awful for you. You have worked so hard for them. You've been there for how long? Five years?"

She shrugs. "I guess that's just the way it is nowadays. Business comes before people. Really, I'm not as upset about it as I could be. I feel poised on the brink of new beginnings." She smiles across the table at Jessie. "Eat your cake."

Jessie smiles, despite herself. "I'm pleased you're taking it that way. Here's to positive new beginnings. I think I'll pass on the cake." She raises her coffee cup in a toast to her sister.

After finishing a second cup of coffee, they walk arm-in-arm out of the coffee shop and back into the sunny afternoon. They stop outside, for a moment, to say their goodbyes and hug each other tightly.

"Keep in touch, Mel. Let me know me know what happens with both your love life and a new job. I know you'll be just fine, but I expect to hear regular updates." Jessie blows a kiss and walks away.

Mel walks to her car and drives home, feeling overstuffed and lethargic. No more scoffing cakes, she tells herself. As Jess said, it is time for new beginnings and perhaps it is the right moment to start a healthy eating and exercise routine, as well. She know she let herself go and now is the perfect time to rein her overeating back in. She decides she will plan out a diet and exercise schedule and she *will* stick to it. She has plenty of time to focus on herself now, with no boyfriend to keep happy and no job.

She drags out her old rebounder trampoline from where it is stored in the garage and sets it up in the lounge room. She looks at it for a moment, before deciding she will not use it just yet. Her health and fitness plan is not starting until tomorrow, after all. No-one ever started a diet in the late afternoon. Instead, she sits down at the computer with a large glass of wine and a bowl of salted nuts and searches Pinterest for diet recipes and exercise plans.

On Sunday morning, she begins the day with a ten-minute bounce on the rebounder, while watching an inane morning TV show. Ten minutes is enough for both the exercise and the television program. She bounces off the mini tramp, exhausted, and staggers to the kitchen for a glass of water. After eating a light mushroom and egg white omelette for breakfast, she takes a 20-minute walk around the block before returning home for a shower. She feels better already, or she would if it was not for her aching calf muscles and hot, sweaty face. She pulls at her clothes, already imagining they feel a little looser, though of course that is impossible.

She spends the morning shopping for her fresh diet ingredients and carries her bags of healthy groceries home triumphantly. She makes herself a large salad for dinner, accompanied by a large glass of chilled water, and slowly eats and savours every mouthful, just as her Pinterest diet plan suggests. After dinner, she pulls on some baggy yoga pants and a pair of walking shoes and sets off to walk around the block again, pushing herself even though her muscles scream *no* and her face feels hot and uncomfortable. She can do this; she knows she can.

She peers at herself in the bathroom mirror before taking a shower. She sucks her cheeks in and looks at herself critically from both sides. Yes, she is looking a little thinner. She can definitely see it. Laughing out loud at her own joke, she steps into the shower. For the first time in a very long while, she feels truly happy.

4

Over the coming weeks, Mel keeps strictly to her diet and exercise plan. She realizes without the ten hour work days, and the slightly stressful date nights with Ben, she can be as obsessive as she chooses about her eating and fitness regime. In addition, she is finally noticing a difference in her body shape. Clothes that had been a little tight before she began her health regime are now hanging loosely off her and zippers which would not zip before now slide up with ease.

Six weeks after beginning her diet, she takes a deep breath as she climbs out of the shower and stands on the scales. She has avoided them until this moment, not wishing to be discouraged by numbers which stubbornly refuse to move. She shuts her eyes, counts to three, and looks down. Then she looks again. She steps off the scales and steps back on again, just to be sure they are working correctly. She has lost 20 pounds. She stares at herself in the bathroom mirror in amazement, noticing her defined cheekbones and the new healthy glow to her face. She accomplished her goal.

Feeling exhilarated, she puts the scales away, gets herself dressed in her too-baggy clothes, and picks up her handbag. A shopping spree is necessary, but nothing too extravagant as she is still unemployed and her redundancy payment will not last for ever. Over the past few weeks, she has focused on her new healthy lifestyle and has not begun to look for work. She knows she has to start the search soon.

She drives to the mall and pops into the hairdressers, where she is able to book a full haircut, blow wave, and lightening treatment for the afternoon, due to an unexpected cancellation. She walks into a trendy fashion boutique and pulls a slinky red dress from the rack. The shop attendant appears beside her. "Is that for you? You have the wrong size. Do you want to try it on? It's a lovely color."

She blushes. Of course, she has not even looked at the size. *What was she thinking, coming into a store like this?* To her amazement, the girl takes the dress from her hands and replaces it with the same dress two sizes smaller.

She looks at the dress, doubtfully. It has been years since she's worn this size. The shopgirl is smiling and looking at her expectantly as she carries the dress into the cubicle, sure that it will not fit. She half expects to hear the sound of fabric tearing as she pulls it over her head, imagining her humiliation when she has to explain to the girl that she ripped it. Instead, she finds that the dress fits beautifully. She stares at herself in the mirror, smoothing the silky fabric down over her hips, scarcely able to believe her new shape. She hardly recognizes herself. Her long-forgotten figure is back at last. A figure she thought she left behind in her teens.

She continues her shopping, delighting in everything she tries on and making several purchases. She stops in at the Food Court for a healthy salad for lunch, and then walks across to the department store to purchase makeup. She has never worn a lot of makeup. Normally, she prefers to be unnoticed and to stay in the background, but propelled by her new confidence she decides she will buy herself some mascara and perhaps even some lip gloss in a scented and lightly pink tone.

"Can I help you?" A shop attendant appears as she looks through the confusingly wide range of mascaras and tries to make a decision on whether she wants long-and-lovely, ultra-curly, or thick-and-luscious lashes.

She smiles uncertainly, with several coloured tubes of mascara clutched in her hand. "I'm just looking for some mascara, and maybe some pale pink lip gloss, if you have any."

The girl peers at her closely, her face alive with interest. "You have such lovely features. Do you usually wear much make up? We have a new product line in. Would you like me to make up your face? I've been wanting to try the samples out on someone."

She looks around, feeling slightly self-conscious. No one is paying her any attention. She looks over to where the girl is pointing to an array of brightly coloured pretty pots, jars, and compacts stacked on the counter. Quickly, before she can change her mind, she nods her head. "Thank you. I would like that."

She watches in amazement as the girl expertly transforms her into someone else entirely. She hardly recognizes the face staring back at her from the well-lit makeup counter mirror.

The girl finishes working and stands back, looking very pleased with the results. "You're beautiful. We have these products discounted as a new line special at present. Would you be interested in buying the products I've used today? They do suit you."

She cannot resist buying the foundation, mascara, eyeshadows, and lipstick on offer. *How can she say no when just ten minutes of work makes her look so lovely?* She winces a little as she hands her credit card over, yet again. Her card has received a battering today, but she does not want to think too much about it. She still has a haircut to pay for. She thanks the girl and takes her purchases before hurrying to her appointment with the hairdresser.

She takes a seat in the chair and the hairdresser asks what she wants done, running her fingers through her hair as she speaks to her in the mirror. She stares at her reflection and the overgrown mousy hair which hangs down past her shoulders. She glances at the poster of a stunning model on the wall and makes a decision. "Short and blonde," she says firmly.

The hairdresser shapes her hair into a cute pixie style and applies the dye solution before handing her a magazine and telling her to relax for a while. She sits back in the chair and flicks through the magazine, feeling very pleased with herself. She cannot remember ever spending this much time or money on herself. It feels good.

By the end of the session, her hair is shaped and blow waved into a shining contemporary blonde style. They both stare admiringly at her reflection as she shakes her head slowly from side-to-side and watches it move and shimmer. She really does look fabulous. Thanking the hairdresser for her work, she leaves the salon and walks through the mall feeling more confident and pretty than she has ever felt before. With her transformation complete, it is now time to get serious about job hunting. She needs to get back into the workforce and make some money to pay her rent as well as today's unexpected credit card blowout. "The vacation is over," she tells herself firmly.

Cherie Mitchell

After searching through listings on an online job site, she applies for several Personal Assistant positions. She feels confident and sure about the positions, and her prior experience makes her suitable for a lot more jobs than she imagined. She pushes send on the last application and logs off her computer to go and complete her exercise workout, a part of her day which she now looks forward to very much.

Two days later, she receives a phone call in response to one of her applications. To her delight, an interview is arranged for the following Monday. Pleased she received such a prompt reply and hopeful of a good outcome, she pulls her new clothes from the wardrobe and begins the very important task of trying on a range of possible interview outfits.

After dressing in a smart black blazer and skirt, with her new makeup applied and her newly blonde hair flicked in a sweeping fringe across her forehead, she looks in the mirror and admits she is impressed. There is no sign of the old Mel in the poised and glowing image smiling back at her. She carefully hangs the clothes back on their hangers, feeling positive and happily expectant about the upcoming interview.

***

She arranges to meet Jessie at the café on the Pier on Saturday morning for coffee and a walk along the beach. She is determined to keep up with her new healthy lifestyle, even when she is socializing. Besides, it is fun to walk and talk. She climbs out of her car and waves at Jessie, who just pulled into a parking spot a short distance away.

Jessie hesitates and stares at her sister in disbelief. "Mel, I nearly didn't recognise you. You look fantastic." Jess hugs her, and then stands back to look at her again, shaking her head. "You've lost so much weight and your hair looks fabulous."

She laughs and shakes her head to allow her hair to move around and fall back into place, knowing that gesture shows the cut to its best effect. "Thank you. I *feel* fabulous." It feels good to receive the compliment and her confidence moves up another small notch. The old hesitant and mousy Mel seems to be very far away in the distance. She is glad. Her new and improved self is definitely a lot more fun.

Cherie Mitchell

Jessie cannot stop staring at her as they walk across the parking lot toward the café. "I'm absolutely amazed, Mel. Who would've thought getting dumped and losing your job meant such an amazing transformation for you? Tell me, have you found a new position yet?"

She tells Jessie about Monday's job interview as they wait at the counter for their coffee, before walking outside to find a table with a view of the ocean and the pier.

"I'm so pleased for you, Mel, and I think you will knock them dead at the interview. You deserve a good job. You deserve the best of everything." She raises her coffee cup. "Best of luck for Monday, and promise you'll let me know as soon as you hear back from them."

After they finish their coffee, they walk down onto the grey sands of the beach and along the shoreline, looking toward the lilac range of mountains far in the distance, while the small waves whisper against the shore. An easterly wind blows off the water, keeping the temperature down. It is a pleasant enough day for walking.

A few hours later, they walk back into the car park and hug goodbye. "Bye, Mel," Jessie calls as she strides across the car park to her car. "Remember to phone me Monday afternoon and let me know how you get on with the job interview."

Monday morning, Mel dresses carefully, applies her makeup just as the girl in the department store did, and blow dries her hair. She glances in the mirror one last time, then picks up her resume folder and walks to the car for the short drive into the city. She is feeling nervous and a little on edge as she pulls into the visitor car park behind the building. It has been many years since her last interview. She feels out of practice and unsure of what lies ahead.

She takes a deep breath and crosses her fingers before walking into the office. The reception area is fresh and bright, with several large potted palms and an upright tropical fish tank in one corner. The girl behind the reception desk is well groomed and professional, but she does not feel out of place or uncomfortable under her steady gaze. The receptionist asks her name, and then asks her to take a seat to wait for Scott, the man who will be conducting the interview.

She picks up one of the latest glossy magazines from the low table in front of her and thumbs through it without seeing anything. Her nervousness is increasing. Her palms feel clammy and her mouth is dry. *What if she fumbles the interview and gives a terrible impression? Is she good enough for the role? Are the other applicants more suitable for the position than she? What if she says the wrong thing?*

"Melody Winters?" A good-looking business-suited man is standing in front of her chair, gazing down at her expectantly. There is something vaguely familiar about him, but for several seconds she cannot put her finger on what it is. With a start, she remembers where she has seen him before. He is the man who caught her when she stumbled and lurched through the door at the restaurant, when her shoe broke, just before Ben dumped her. Scott shows no sign of recognition as he greets her with a professional smile. She stands up and holds out her hand. "Hi, I'm pleased to meet you."

The interview goes exceptionally well. Scott explains he needs a new Personal Assistant urgently, as his previous employee, June, left suddenly due to a family illness. He flicks through her resume, takes note of Cary's phone number in order to get a verbal reference, and asks her several questions about her previous job experience. She feels comfortable talking to him and the job appears to be just what she is looking for. At the end of the interview, he tells her he will be making a decision very quickly, as he hopes to have the successful candidate begin the following Monday. He promises he will phone her with his decision by the end of the day.

She leaves the building feeling confident about her chances of winning the job. *Surely, it is hers?* Scott reacted well to her answers and he seemed impressed by what she told him. She drives home and changes into her exercise clothes. She decides to take her mind off waiting for the call by going for a walk.

Just before five, her mobile finally rings with a call from Scott. By this time, she is beginning to doubt her earlier confidence that the job is hers. However, she can tell by the tone of his voice that he is ringing with good news.

"I think you will be perfect for the role," he says. "I have a feeling we'll work well together." He remindss her of the salary and asks if she is happy with it. "Can you start Monday?"

She is delighted. She hangs up and dials Jessie straight away. "Jess," she cries as soon as her sister picks up. "I got the job. The company sounds really interesting. The building is new and bright. My new boss is gorgeous. The hours are reasonable and the wage is great. I start Monday. It's perfect. Can you believe it?"

"Mel, I'm so happy for you. I'm glad everything worked out just as you hoped. See, I told you this is a great time for new beginnings."

The girls talk a little longer before they say their goodbyes and hang up. Mel is unable to wipe the smile from her face. Her life has taken a turn for the better, and her future suddenly seems brighter.

5

Monday morning, Mel arrives at work at eight-fifteen, dressed in one of her new professional outfits and ready to begin her new job. The reception area is empty when she walks in, and the faint smell of cleaning products hangs in the air. She walks through the building to Scott's office. The door is half ajar and she can see him working at his desk. He looks up at her knock and gives her a dazzling smile. "Mel, good to see you, again, come on in. You're here early. You're lucky I am already in and the building is unlocked. No one else starts until right at eight-, so please don't worry about coming in any earlier in future. I don't expect my employees to work outside their paid hours. Come and sit down and I'll show you what I'd like you to start on this morning."

She sits in the chair opposite Scott and listens to him explain the parts of the role he needs addressed most urgently. June has been gone for two weeks now, and the typing and travel bookings have fallen behind. Scott tells her he is keen for her getting him organized again, as he has a busy and often complicated schedule. It is clear he relies heavily on his Personal Assistant and already she is itching to get started in the role. She watches him as he describes his schedule, noting the way a stray dark curl falls forward onto his forehead in a charming and distracting way whenever he moves his head. He looks at her directly as he speaks and she realizes how she can easily be lost in those hazel eyes if she does not keep herself focused. He really is a very appealing man. A little too appealing for someone who is going to be her boss. *How is a girl supposed to get her work done with a man like that sitting just a few feet away from her desk?*

Half an hour later, Scott hands her a stack of papers and asks her to come and meet the rest of the staff. He introduces her to Kasey, at the front desk; Tim, the accountant; Louise, the payroll and accounts lady; and his business partner, Jack. Everyone is very welcoming and friendly, and she already feels at home here in the office.

Scott shows her to the desk she will be using outside his office and asks her to check with Kasey for June's log-on and passwords. He shows her his appointment book and tells her June was quite old school in her habits, preferring to keep manual records. He assumes she might prefer to

Cherie Mitchell

use the Outlook calendar. Nodding at the pile of papers, he asks if she can type them up as soon as possible. H The e assures her she should not hesitate to ask him any questions, and then he leaves her to it.

The morning passes quickly and Mel discovers she enjoys being back in the office routine. In some ways it feels as if she never had any time off at all, although she is a different person from the girl who worked for Cary. Trimmer, more confident, and happier. She smiles at the thought and returns to her work.

At one o'clock, Scott pokes his head around the door of his office and reminds her she should take a lunch break. He tells her he will be out of the office for the remainder of the afternoon and he has his mobile with him if she needs anything.

She picks up her bag, amused that Scott is insisting she take a lunch break. Cary barely noticed if she took the time to grab herself a coffee. Louise from payroll and accounts catches up with her as she is walking out the door. "Are you going out to get some lunch? Do you want to walk with me? There is a coffee shop just up the road, but it isn't very good. There's a much better one around the corner. I can show you where it is."

"That would be lovely. I don't really know the area." She falls into step with her new colleague.

"How are you finding the new job? Don't you think Scott is utterly drop dead gorgeous?" Louise is around her age, short, with a no-nonsense haircut, and a wide, welcoming smile. Her enthusiasm over Scott is evident.

She laughs. "The job is going well, and yes, I have to agree with you Scott is a very good-looking man."

They bought sandwiches and cold drinks at the coffee shop. Louise points up the street toward a little grassy reserve area, complete with a bench seat and several small trees. "We can go over there, if you like. I come down here often on warm days. It's just good to get away from the office for a while and clear my head."

They reach the grassy area and sit on the park bench to eat their lunches. Louise tells her about her husband, Cameron, and their little girl Elisa. Her pride in them clear in her voice. She says she places Elisa in day care during the day, which works out well for everyone. She says Cameron is a builder, with a keen interest in his weekend hobby of go-karts. She rolls her eyes as she says it, but Mel can tell she is not really annoyed. "Boys and their toys. Most Sundays you'll find us down at the go-kart track." She changes the subject, suddenly, and asks Mel if she has a husband or partner.

"No. Not at the moment. For now, I'm single and I'm surprised to find myself enjoying the single life. I've always had a boyfriend, so I thought I would hate being by myself, but I've found it to be a positive experience. I've spent the time since Ben and I broke up getting fit and healthy and I'm pleased with the results. I'm happier and healthier than I have been in years." She stretches her legs out in the warmth of the sun and feels a bubble of happiness well up inside her. She realizes everything she just said is true. *Why hadn't she realized this sooner instead of tying herself into unsatisfactory and unfulfilling relationships?*

Louise nods, apparently pleased with her comments. "It's always good to spend time on yourself. I don't get much chance, but when I do, I definitely make the most of it. You're very attractive. I don't expect you'll be single for much longer."

"Thank you." She smiles at the compliment, but really, a new relationship is the last thing on her mind. She

Cherie Mitchell ·

unwraps her sandwich and sinks her teeth into the soft wholemeal bread, spicy chicken, and crunchy salad. It is a beautiful day, she just commenced a new job she knows she is going to enjoy, and it seems she made a new friend. *Can life get any better?*

***

Mel's first week passes quickly. Scott is in and out of the office all day and when he is onsite, he often holds meetings, which he asks her to attend in order to take the minutes. Her job involves a lot of appointment making, typing, and a large amount of research. She meets Louise for lunch most days and they stroll down to the little park to eat. She finds herself enjoying Louise and an easy friendship is forming between them.

Friday morning, she is engrossed in typing the minutes from the previous day's meeting and trying to decipher her own handwriting. Scott is in his office and she knows he will be leaving, shortly. She can see on his Outlook calendar he has a lunch date with "SB," an entry he made himself. She has just typed the final bullet point when she hears the entrance door to the office open and a woman's voice in the reception talking with Kasey. She does not pay too much attention.

Suddenly she looks up to see a tall, thin, and extremely beautiful brunette standing in front of her desk with a discontented scowl marring her pretty face. "Who are you?" she demands without introduction. "Where is June?"

"Hello. I'm Mel, Scott's new Personal Assistant. June has retired and I started work here on Monday." She smiles at the girl. "Can I help you with anything?"

The girl glares at her and spins on her heel. Her long, glossy hair twirls around her. She pushes the door to Scott's office open without knocking.

She quickly stands up. "Excuse me. Can I help? Scott is not expecting a visitor."

The girl ignores her and pushes the door shut behind her. It does not shut completely so she can clearly hear the conversation. Her voice is raised and angry. She does not sound as if she is in any mood for explanations.

"Scott, you didn't tell me June left. You knew I'd like to have that job. I can't believe you hired someone without even telling me. Who is she? Her hair is too blonde and her top is too low. She's practically got her boobs out on display for everyone who walks in. I don't like her."

"Stacey." She can hear Scott's reply. His voice is low, and steady, and dangerous. "Keep your voice down, please." The door to the office is quickly pushed shut with a click and she can no longer hear a word.

She glances down at the top she is wearing. She does not think it is too low. In fact, Louise told her this morning how professional she looked, and it is not as if she is well endowed in the breast department, anyway. It is a bit extreme for someone who spoke with her for all of thirty seconds to announce she does not like her. She feels more than a little put out as she does up the buttons on her blouse right to the top.

A few minutes later, the door to Scott's office re-opens and he and the girl walk out. He stops in front of her desk and rests his hand causally on the polished wood. "Mel, I'd like you to meet my girlfriend, Stacey. Stacey, this is Mel, June's replacement." He smiles across the desk at her, his hazel eyes warm. She smiles back, glad of his unspoken support, before she says hello to Stacey. Stacey sniffles and says nothing, instead choosing to examine her glossy red manicure.

Scott takes Stacey's arm and steers her out of the office, calling back to Mel as he does so. "I'm going to be at lunch until two, and then I have another appointment. I will be at a twilight golf meeting with Dave from Smiths & Webster after that. I won't be back in the office today. Please feel free to leave a little early when you finish all you need to get done. Have a good weekend and thanks for all your help this week, Mel."

He puts his hand on the small of Stacey's back and steers her through reception, out the front door, and into the car park. She stares after them. *Scott is so nice. What is he doing with the very rude Stacey? He can do so much better.* She shrugs, deciding there is no accounting for taste, and goes back to her work.

6

Mel finishes her work by 3:45 and packs up her desk. She enjoyed her first week on the job and is looking forward to returning to the office next week. She feels lucky to have found a position with this company and is sure it is the beginning of an interesting new career. Except for her brief meeting with Stacey, everything has gone very well.

She picks up her handbag and stops at Louise's office on her way out. "Bye Louise. I've finished for the week and Scott said I could leave early. Have a great weekend."

Louise looks up from her desk and smiles at her friend. She pushes her straight, mousy-brown hair behind her ears and Mel thinks she suddenly looks very young, too young to be the mother of a busy pre-schooler. "You have a good weekend, too. Did you meet the lovely Stacey? I heard her voice in reception earlier and made sure I avoided her. I bet she hated you on sight."

She laughs. "Yes, I did meet her, and yes she didn't hesitate to tell Scott she doesn't like me. She didn't say it in front of me, of course, but the door to his office was open and I heard her. She is very beautiful, though."

Louise shakes her head. "Beauty is only skin deep. Watch out, she will see you as a threat because you are so gorgeous. She is the insanely jealous type, so make sure you keep out of her way as much as possible. She is very insecure and they are always the worst kind."

"Thanks Louise, and I will take your advice. I'll see you next week." She walks through reception and out into the warm afternoon.

She drives home, changes into her exercise gear, and takes the winding road up to the Port Hills. She parks in Victoria Park and walks along Ell's Track, toward the summit. It is a beautiful, clear afternoon, with only a few wisps of clouds in the sky and the faintest of breezes stirring the leaves of the surrounding trees. She breathes deeply and feels the tension ease away. She loves being up here, above the city, in the fresh air and openness.

She walks around a bend in the track and sees a man leaning against an outcrop of rock to one side of the path, his back stoops as he studies his ankle. He looks up as she approaches and she notes a look of pain on his face.

"Is everything okay?"

He frowns at his ankle as he rubs his hand over it. "I think so. I wrenched my ankle on a loose stone. For a moment, I thought I sprained it, but it's just twisted, I think. Hopefully, it'll come right in a few minutes." He puts the foot down on the path and stands up carefully, testing his weight on the injured ankle. He takes a few cautious steps and smiles back over his shoulder at her.

"It's fine, no pain at all." He gives her an interested look, his eyes skimming over her t-shirt and shorts, down her legs, and back to her face. "Hi, I'm Mark. It's a beautiful day to be up here."

"I'm Mel." She returns his smile. He is tall and fit-looking, with sun-bleached hair and cute dimples. His cornflower blue eyes twinkle when he smiles and she suddenly feels a little shy. He falls into step beside her as she continues walking up the track.

"I walk up here all the time," he says. "At the risk of sounding corny, do you come here often?"

She giggles. "I come up here as much as possible. I'm usually at work at this time, but my boss gave me an early day and I decided to make the most of it. It's my first week in a new job and I'm really loving it. What do you do, Mark?"

He tells her he manages his own printing business, a company he built up from scratch. He usually finishes work early on Fridays to make the most of walking or hiking in the fresh air before the weekend arrives and all the hikers and families crowd the trails. They chat easily as they continue following the winding trail around the side of the hills. Mel is engrossed in their conversation and surprised when they reach the summit car park without barely noticing how far they walked.

"My car is parked up here," Mark says. "Where did you park?"

She points back down the hill. "Mine's down in Victoria Park. I better turn around and head back. Thanks for your company, Mark. I hope your ankle doesn't give you any more grief."

Mark hesitates for a moment. "You're probably married or happily partnered up, but if you aren't, can I interest you in a coffee or a drink sometime? Maybe tomorrow if you aren't busy?" He grins at her. "I'm half expecting you to say no, but if I don't ask, I'll kick myself as soon as you disappear from sight."

She does not think twice. "I would love to. No, I don't have a husband or partner. Yes, tomorrow would be perfect."

They exchange mobile numbers and make a date for a drink on Saturday afternoon at the Stag's Head. She waves and walks back down the hill toward her car, smiling to herself. Mark intrigues her and she is interested in getting to know him better. She wonders if he would have asked the old Mel out, but then she pushes that thought away. The new Mel is here to stay and the old Mel no longer exists.

***

Saturday afternoon, Mel changes into her favourite jeans and a light blue floral top before driving over to meet Mark at the Stag's Head. He is already at the pub when she arrives, seated at an outdoor table with a glass of beer in front of him. He stands up and kisses her cheek. Dressed in a t-shirt and jeans he's looking even more handsome than he did on the walking track. "Good to see you. Take a seat and I'll get you a drink. What will you have?"

"Wine thanks, white. Either sauvignon or chardonnay, I don't mind." She watches him walk over to the bar. The jeans fit around his bum well, with no hint of a sag in the pants seat. His blonde-tipped hair just grazes the top of his collar, his shoulders are broad, and he carries himself with a quiet confidence. *Nice.*

He comes back with her glass of wine and raises his glass in a toast. "Here's to chance meetings on mountain tracks." He displays a devilish grin.

The afternoon passes quickly and they never even begin to run out of conversation. Mark is attentive and funny and interesting, as well as very attractive. He holds Mel's gaze, asks pertinent questions in just the right places, and answers anything she asks him without hedging around as Ben would have.

It seems that time has stood still when he looks at his watch. "Can you believe it's six o'clock already? Do you want to make a night of it and go on somewhere else for drinks and dinner?"

She nods. "I'd love to." She too is surprised at the time, but does not want their meeting to end. Not yet. She already knows she likes Mark a lot. He is *definitely* boyfriend material.

They walk up the street to an Italian restaurant and dawdle over pizza and conversation, have a few more drinks, and suddenly it is close to 10:00.

"After all these drinks, I'll be taking a cab home and collecting my car tomorrow," Mel says as she reaches for her handbag.

"Taxi with me to my place. We'll have a coffee and sit on the deck, and look at the stars and talk some more."

She pauses for only a minute before agreeing. She still does not want the night to end. "That sounds like a great idea."

Mark's house is a big, sprawling property, all wooden boards and shutters, with a large rambling garden at the front. He notices her surprise when she comments on the size of the house. "I know, it's a big house just for one person, but I share it with my dog, Rastus, and honestly, it was such a bargain when I was looking for a property that I just had to buy it. Come on in and have a look around." He unlocks the door and shows her around, pointing out work he has already completed and telling her of his plans for future renovations. He introduces her to Rastus, a small terrier who is clearly devoted to Mark, and then makes them both a coffee.

They sit on old, wooden chairs on the back deck with Rastus at their feet and the stars overhead. Everything fees comfortable and natural, and when he leans over and kisses her, she kisses him right back. He pulls her to her feet and holds her close, kissing her deeply. She sinks into him, exploring his mouth with her tongue. He tastes like fresh air, sunshine, and beer. After a few minutes, he pulls away and raises an eyebrow at her. "Bed?"

She hesitates and pulls back a little. "I'm not a one-night stand type of girl."

He bends and kisses her again. She feels her body respond to his caresses. She is mellow and relaxed after their afternoon of sunshine and wine, and he smells fantastic.

"Who said it would be just a one-night stand?" He whispers against her mouth.

She allows her body to win the argument and lets him to lead her inside. They walk through the house to his bedroom and fall onto the bed, still kissing. He pushes her hair back off her face and gazes into her eyes. "You're beautiful," he whispers. He places a hand on her breast. She sighs. *It has been too long.*

He helps her remove her top and begins to kiss and lick her nipples, sucking hard and then lapping in slow circles. She arches her back in pleasure and a small moan escapes. He raises his head and looks at her face. "Take all your clothes off," he whispers. "I want to look at all of you."

She feels confident in her nakedness. She knows her body is fit and strong and she looks good. She quickly undresses, feeling his eyes on her and revelling in his admiration. His cock is hard and erect. She reaches for it as he begins to kiss her again. He moves slowly down her body, kissing a line from her lips, across her breasts, and down her belly. He looks up and grins before pushing his face into her pussy and circling her clit in exquisite slow motion. She cries out and twines her hands into his hair. He pushes a finger inside her as he continues to lap and gently suck. Within minutes, she bursts into orgasm.

He moves slowly back up her body, kissing a tantalizing line over her stomach and breasts before nuzzling his face into her neck. "You came. You taste wonderful." He watches her face as he thrusts his penis deep inside her. She gasps and wraps her legs around his back, pulling him in closer. He fucks her, slow and hard, never taking his eyes from hers. She can feel herself drowning in his gaze and she cannot look away, mesmerized by the desire she sees reflected there. She reaches down and rubs her clit, bringing herself to orgasm again as he thrust himself in and out of her, filling her entirely his cock. He finally groans and gives himself up to his own orgasm. He falls on the bed beside her and pulls her into his arms. He kisses her hair and face, his breath hot on her skin. "Do you feel good?" he murmurs.

She smiles happily and snuggles into him. "I do feel good." She feels sleepy, happy, and *wanted*.

In the morning, they wake up still entwined with each other. He leans across and kisses her on the mouth, gently pulling at her lower lip with his teeth. "Good morning, beautiful. Mmmm, I'm so glad I twisted my ankle on that trail, otherwise I might never have met you."

She turns into him, reaching for his cock again. "Me too. Do you want me to show you how pleased I am?"

His penis responds instantly, hard and hot and eager. He groans and lies back as she bends down to take his cock in her mouth, flicking her tongue over the tip of his penis while she runs her hand up and down his shaft. He allows her to work on him for a few minutes, moaning his appreciation, before he pushes her away, flips her over, and holds himself above her. "You're driving me mad." He reaches down and strokes his hands over her inner thighs, teasing her by getting close but not close enough. She grabbed at his hand and pushes it onto her clit. He laughs and begins to rub her in tiny delicious circles.

She feels the sensations building inside her again and just as she was about to cum, he plunges his cock inside her without warning, pressing his pubic bone against her clit as he moves rapidly against her. She cries out and clutches his shoulders as wave after wave of orgasm surges through her. He groans and quickly follows with his own orgasm before collapsing against her. "My God, you're amazing."

She rests her head against his chest. She can hear his heart beating, rhythmic and soothing, and she feels warm and utterly desirable. She wraps her arms around him and sinks, once again, into a peaceful doze.

She is jolted awake by the beep of a text message. She opens her eyes, disorientated and unsure of where she is for a moment. She watches through half-closed eyes as Mark reaches for his phone and looks at the screen. As he does so, a second text message beeps. He quickly switches the phone off and places it back on his bedside table.

"Is anything the matter?" she asks, sleepily.

"No, it's nothing." He reaches for her again, pulling her into his arms and kissing her like he really means it.

Later, they eat a leisurely breakfast on the deck, comfortable and at ease in each other's company. Rastus runs around the rambling lawn, snapping at swooping dragonflies and butterflies. It is a perfect summer Sunday morning and she cannot remember a time she felt happier.

He kisses her again, while she waits for an Uber to come collect her and take her to her car. "Thanks for a fantastic night." He gives her another one of his deep, searching looks. "I'll give you a call during the week. Maybe we can meet for dinner on Thursday night, if you're free?"

"I would love to. I'll speak to you soon." She climbs into the Uber, feeling rosy and utterly sure her life has, once again, taken a turn for the better. *Surely, it is Fate that brought them together on her favourite mountain track?*

7

Mel washes a load of laundry Sunday night and gives the house a quick tidy and clean before making herself a light salad for dinner. She cannot stop smiling as she thinks about the night she spent with Mark. She decides to ring Jessie, suddenly needing to share her happiness with her sister.

"Hi Jess," she sings as her sister answers the phone.

"Mel! Hang on a minute. I'll just give Jayden to his Dad." She waits as Jessie hands her baby son to her husband, Ricky. She listens to the happy family chatter in the background for a few minutes, idly drawing circles with her finger on the arm of the sofa, before Jessie comes back on the phone.

"What's up, Mel? How did your first week at work go?"

She tells Jessie about her week, her lunches with Louise, and how excited she is to have landed such a great job. "And," she pauses for effect, "I met someone lovely, I stayed over at his place last night, and I'm meeting him again for dinner on Thursday."

Jessie squeals into the phone. "Mel, that's fantastic. I'm so pleased for you. Come on, give me the details, I want all the gossip. I'm an old, married lady and I don't get to have these kind of adventures anymore. What's he like?"

She smiles. She does not have to be asked twice. She tells Jessie all about Mark and the night they spent together, only stopping when she hears Jayden crying in the background. "Jess, I'll let you go now and tend to my gorgeous nephew. I just wanted to tell you that everything is perfect in my world. I'll talk to you soon."

***

Monday morning, Mel bounces out of bed, full of the joys of living. She showers and dresses, fluffs up her fabulous hairstyle, applies her makeup, and drives to work, singing along to the tunes on the car radio all the way to the city.

"Hi Kasey," she beams at the young receptionist as she skips toward her desk. She hums as she sits down and logs onto her computer. She taps her foot happily as she checks Scott's calendar for the day and reads through the new emails in her inbox. Next, she reads through the Post-It notes Scott left on her keyboard, the lyrics of a love song playing through her head. She books a return flight for Scott's trip later in the week, and makes an appointment for his haircut on Wednesday, while she pictures Mark's face. She flags a note to herself to phone Steven Murphy's PA later in the day to make a dinner appointment for Scott and Stephen on Wednesday evening, while doodling a heart on her desk pad. She emails Scott his flight details and the itinerary for the Auckland trip, while humming yet more love song lyrics. She then forces herself to focus and begins typing the agenda for the first meeting of the day.

Scott arrives just after 9.30. "Hi Mel, did you have a good weekend?"

She smiles back. Her boss really does have the most engaging smile, but it is nothing like Mark's, of course. "I had a lovely weekend, thank you, Scott. How about you?"

"It was great." He walks into his office and then pops his head back out again. "Can I read the agenda for the 11.00 meeting once you've finished typing it up? Thanks, Mel."

The first meeting finishes on time, at twelve-thirty. She quickly reads over the notes she took when she returns to her desk, correcting the words that look slightly indecipherable before she forgets what she wrote. She checks her phone, hoping for a text from Mark. Nothing, which is a little disappointing. She checks the time. The next meeting is not until two, so she can stop for lunch. She picks up her bag and walks down the hall to Louise's office.

"Hi Louise, I haven't had a chance to catch up with you yet. It's been a crazy busy morning. Do you want to walk down to the café and grab a sandwich with me?" She pauses, peering at the other woman closely. "Louise, is there something wrong?"

Louise sniffles and dabs at her eyes. "No, it's just a cold. I might finish up here soon and head on home. I'll go straight to bed and Cameron can collect Elisa from day-care once he's finished work." She holds her hand up, warning Mel to keep her distance. "Don't come any closer. You don't want to catch my bug."

She takes a step back. "Don't worry, I'm as healthy as a bean sprout. I'm sure I won't catch it. You take care of yourself and I'll see you once you're back at work. You should go home now. You're of no use to anyone in this state and there's no sense in spreading your germs around the office."

Louise nods, a tissue held to her nose as she bends to pick up her handbag. "You're right. I'll leave now. Hopefully I'll sleep it off and be back at work tomorrow. See you, Mel."

Mel walks down to the coffee shop to buy a salad and sandwich to eat at her desk, bypassing the reserve for today. She eats her lunch and returns to her typing. By the time the attendees begin arriving for the meeting, she has typed up the minutes from the first meeting and prepared the agenda for meeting number two.

As the meeting wraps up, Scott asks the other attendees if they will come with him for an off-site visit to one of the subsidiary plants. He glances across the board table at her. "Can you have the second lot of minutes ready for me when I return? Just leave them on my desk when you're done. I know that you leave at four-thirty, but I won't be back by then. I've got the feeling this visit might take a while."

After the men leave, she clears the water glasses and coffee cups from the boardroom table. She rinses the glasses and crockery, and tidies up the room before picking up her notes and walking up the hallway toward her desk.

As she passes Louise's office, an unexpected movement catches her eye. She stops in surprise. Louise had gone home long ago and there should not be anyone in her office. Everyone knows the payroll office is off limits. She peers in the door and is startled to see Stacey sitting at Louise's computer. "Oh, hi Stacey. Scott has just gone off-site. He won't be back until after five. Louise has gone home sick, and she didn't tell me that you'd be in. Can I help you with anything?"

Stacey jumps, clearly surprised to be interrupted. Her eyes narrow and her mouth tightens into a grim line when she sees her. "No, you can't help me. I'm just looking for something."

Everything feels wrong. Stacey is Scott's girlfriend, not an employee, and she has no business poking around in Louise's office when neither Louise nor Scott are in the building. Making up her mind, she steps into the office and stands firmly in front of the desk. "That's fine, Stacey, but if I can't help you, I'm sure Jack or Tim can. Should I just go and find one of them for you?"

Stacey abruptly stands up, quickly closing the lid of Louise's laptop. "That won't be necessary." She brushes roughly past Mel and strides toward the door. "I know my way around here and I certainly don't need my boyfriend's PA giving me orders." She stops in the doorway and looks Mel up and down, her lip curls. "By the way, I don't think your outfit is entirely appropriate for the corporate image this company maintains."

She flounces off and hears the entrance door slam behind her. She looks down at her outfit. She is wearing a crisp, white shirt and a short-ish black skirt with black court shoes. The skirt is perhaps a little brief, but it stops just above her knees. Her legs are tan and muscular. Her skirt is certainly longer than Kasey's, whose barely covers her arse. She dismisses Stacey's comment and walks back to her desk to begin typing the minutes. She has work to do and is not about to let Stacey, and her catty comments, get to her.

***

Cherie Mitchell

Mel finds herself checking her mobile phone several times over the course of the evening. She expected to hear from Mark by now and is surprised she has not even received a text, given the wonderful night they spent together. She pushes her phone aside and tells herself not to be impatient. He told her he'd call her and she is sure he will. She smiles again at the memory of what they shared, both the conversation and the sex. Yes, he will call her, she is sure of it.

When she arrives at work the next day, she stops for a moment at the reception desk to talk to Kasey. "Does Stacey come into the offices very often?" She keeps her voice casual. It would not do to make a fuss if Stacey is a regular fixture in the office.

"Sometimes she comes in a couple of times a week and sometimes it's a month until we see her again." Kacey fixes her ponytail and reaches for her lip gloss to reapply another coat, concentrating on the little mirror she pulls from her purse.

Mel nods. Kasey does not seem concerned that Stacey was in the office, so it seems it is nothing to worry about. "Is Louise in today?"

"Yeah, she arrived just before you. She should be in her office."

She walks down the hallway to Louise's office and pops her head around the door. "Hey, you. How are you feeling today?"

Louise gives her a watery smile. Her nose is red, but she looks a little brighter than the day before. "I'm a little tired, but overall I'm much better. I think Elisa is coming down with it now. I sent her to day-care this morning, but I'm half-expecting them to call and ask me to come and get her."

"Well, let me know if you have to leave." She starts to walk away and then turns back as a thought strikes her. "Louise, did you log out of your computer yesterday when you left?"

Louise looks confused. "I really couldn't tell you. I felt so ill I wasn't paying close attention." She opens her computer. "I must not have. I'm still logged on."

Mel bites her lip, knowing she has to say something. "Is there any reason Stacey would need to be in your office looking at your work?"

Louise looks surprised. "Stacey? Scott's girlfriend? No, there is no reason at all. She doesn't work here and doesn't have anything to do with what goes on in my office. Why would you ask me that?"

Mel watches her face carefully, as she tells her she saw Stacey sitting at her desk after she went home and after Scott left the building.

"Watch out for her, Mel. She thinks she owns this place. I don't think there is anything she could have found on my computer, but..." Louise quickly scans her emails. "It doesn't make me feel good to know she was snooping around my desk."

Mel walks to her desk feeling uneasy. She will make sure she logs out whenever she is away from her desk from now on. She does not trust Stacey either. She logs on and reads through her emails. Scott sent her an early morning message with the details of an important new proposal. She reads through the notes. The transaction is top secret and highly confidential, as one of their biggest competitors is chasing the same client they are. He lists the scope of the proposal, the forecast budget, and the names of all interested or involved parties. He wants her to type the document and states (underlined in red) it is essential this information is treated as confidential and not be distributed to anyone else.

As she scans the list of businesses and companies involved in the deal, she stops on one name and smiles when she recognizes Mark's printing company. If this deal goes ahead, it will mean a lot of work for him, *and a* lot of extra money. She wonders again when she will hear from him. She thinks he should have at least texted her by now and feels a tiny prickle of dread. She does not know him well despite what they did together. *Was it only a one-night stand, regardless of what he said?*

Scott rushes into the office just before ten. His business jacket is unbuttoned and there is a smear of grease on his cheek. "Mel, can you organize a hire car and drop me off to collect it? My car is broke down and I have the busiest of days ahead." He glances at his watch as he continues on past her desk. "I have an important meeting at ten-forty-five. Can you phone and organize the rental? If we leave in five minutes and collect the car I should be make it on time. Thanks."

She drops Scott off to collect the hire car, assuring him if he needs anything else he should give her a call. The traffic is busy and the errand takes longer than expected, but she reminds herself a PA should be used to handling unexpected disruptions to her day. She stops at a lunch bar on the way back to work and picks up a salad. She has the feeling she might not get the chance to leave her desk again before the day is over.

As she walks into the office, Kasey glances up with a brief "Hi" and goes back to her work. She goes straight to her desk and sits down to begin typing Scott's notes and the proposal specifications.

8

Mel is engrossed in her work when Louise walks out of her office. "Mel, I have to leave. The day-care just called and Elisa is really sick." She glances at the open door of Scott's office. "Is Scott not here? I could've sworn I saw Stacey walk past earlier."

She shakes her head, her attention focused on her typing. "No, he's not here. I dropped him off to pick up a rental car earlier. I haven't seen Stacey". She looks up and gives Louise a sympathetic smile. "Sorry about your daughter. I hope Elisa gets better soon."

Louise looks harassed and worried as she swings her bag over her shoulder and hurries off. "Me too."

Mel eats her salad at her desk and finishes the proposal. She saves it to Scott's drive and emails him the link, pleased the task is finished. She looks through the remainder of her emails and continues working until four-thirty. Kasey is leaving as she walks into the reception on her way out.

"Bye, Mel," Kasey calls as she hurries out the door and climbs onto the back of a revving motorbike, hitching her short skirt up even higher and wrapping her arms around the leather-jacketed rider.

She follows her out, allowing the door to swing shut behind her. Today has been busy and she is looking forward to taking a walk and winding down. *Maybe tonight Mark will text or call. Or perhaps she should send him a casual text, just to make contact? Who said that a woman has to wait for a man to call?*

After dinner, she checks her phone, again. She still has not heard from Mark and it does not make any sense. They had gotten along so well. She decisively types a quick text. "How's your week going? Still on 4 Thursday?" Satisfied, she sends the message and places the phone down on the coffee table. She watches it for several minutes, expecting a reply. When he has not replied by bedtime, she sighs and switches the phone off for the night. She did expect this.

Mel sleeps restlessly, unable to get Mark out of her head. *Why hasn't he contacted her?* In the middle of the night, she sits up in bed and switches on her phone, checking to see if he texted a reply after she switched her phone off. There is still no message.

Cherie Mitchell

She feels tired and listless the next morning. *Maybe Mark sees her as a one-night stand after all? Perhaps he used that one-night stand line on all his conquests?* She did not feel as though he saw their connection as just a hook up, but then again, she does not have a very good track record when it comes to judging men's characters. She stands under the shower for a long time, her face raised to the hot water, trying to rinse off all traces of her sleepless night and her growing disquiet.

She arrives at work and walks to Louise's office. Her desk and chair are empty and the office has a vacant air about it. Elisa is probably still ill. She goes to her desk, noticing that Scott's door is shut. She sits down in her chair and switches on her computer just as Scott opens his door.

"Mel," he says curtly. "Please come into my office. Don't bother starting anything. I'd like to see you straight away." He marches back to his desk, leaving the door open.

She is surprised. Scott has never spoken to her curtly before. She follows him into his office, remembering her final meeting with Cary.

"Shut the door behind you," Scott says. "Please take a seat."

She sits down, feeling distinctly uncomfortable. Scott places his hands on his desk and looks directly at her, his eyebrows lowered. "Mel, I think I made it very clear to you when you took the position of my Personal Assistant that you would have full access to my business life. I expected you to treat that trust with the confidentiality it deserves. Yesterday, when I gave you the scope and the budget for this latest multi-million-dollar proposal I thought I made it very clear, once again, that it is confidential information. Am I correct?"

"Of course." She is confused. She knows a PA has access to a wide range of sensitive business and personal information and she prides herself on her confidentiality. She has no idea where Scott is heading with his questions, but she does not like the direction in which they are going.

"It appears the information I emailed yesterday was forwarded to our competitors. It was forwarded from your email address."

She gasps and gapes at him in horror. She did not send that information anywhere.

"I think you will agree this is an act of gross misconduct. Louise will ensure you receive your wages for the hours you worked. That is all, Mel. Please collect your things and leave the building immediately."

She stares at him, unable to believe what she just heard. Her voice stutters and stumbles as she attempts to defend herself. "Scott, I have no idea what you mean. I typed all the data you gave me into a Word document and saved it to your drive. The only email I sent in relation to the proposal was an email to you to let you know the work was complete. I did not even print any of the documents. I am well aware of the confidentiality of this information. I did not send it anywhere. You have to believe me."

Scott shakes his head. "I'm sorry Mel, but I have a copy of the email containing all the private information, sent to our competitor from your email address." He passes the printed page across the desk. The email is from her address, complete with her automatic signature at the bottom. "I'm not sure why you would do such a thing and I must admit I'm very disappointed. I thought we were building a good relationship. We have nothing more to discuss." He stands up and glowers at her. "Do I need to call Jack to escort you from the building?"

"That won't be necessary. I can see myself out." She stands up on legs which feel like jelly. "I am innocent, I swear it. I did not send that email and I have no idea how it was sent."

She walks out of Scott's office, fighting back tears. *How can this be happening to her?* She picks up her handbag and walks blindly out the door. She climbs into her car, the tears flowing now, and drives straight to Port Hills, to Victoria Park, without even thinking about where she is going. She sits in her car in the parking lot, staring across the plains, trying to make sense of it all. Finally, she picks up her phone.

"Mel, what's wrong?" her sister asks urgently as soon as she speaks.

She bursts into noisy tears. "I just got fired and I have no idea why. I have been accused of something I know nothing about." She sobs loudly and hiccups. "I love that job."

"Hush...take a deep breath. Don't rush. Tell me when you're ready," Jessie soothes, as if she is speaking to Jayden.

She takes a deep breath, then another, focusing on calming her heartbeat. Her sobs gradually quiet and she explains the events of the morning to Jessie.

"But...I don't get it." Jessie is clearly puzzled and struggling to make sense of it herself. "How was the email sent if you didn't send it? Let me get this straight. Your boss emailed you the information, and you were supposed to type it up, then you saved it to his drive, then you emailed him to tell him it was done? Is that it? Is there anything you missed? Did you leave your desk at all? Could you have accidently hit send?"

"No, I couldn't have accidently hit send. I do know what I'm doing." She pauses as an awful thought strikes her. "Oh. Oh, Jess. I had to leave the office to drop Scott off to pick up a rental car and I left my desk. I didn't log off before I left. Oh my God. Stacey."

"What? Who is Stacey?" Jessie asks sharply. "You're not making any sense."

She feels sick. "Stacey is Scott's girlfriend. Scott is my boss. Stacey hated me on sight from the first moment she met me. She was envious because she hoped to be handed the Personal Assistant position if it ever became available.

Louise told me to watch out for her. That she's the insecure and jealous type. I caught her sitting at Louise's desk yesterday after she went home sick. Oh God, Jess. Stacey sent the email and set me up. I just know it."

"You have to tell Scott. You have to. You have to clear your name and get your job back." Jessie's voice is firm.

"But, I don't have any proof. I didn't even see Stacey at the office yesterday. I know it was her, it can't be anyone else, but there is nothing at all to link her to sending that email."

"What about the receptionist? Can she verify Stacey came in while you were gone?"

"I'll ask her," she says. "But I still have no proof Stacey sent the email." She feels trapped. She'd been framed and she can do absolutely nothing about it.

"You have to do all you can to clear your name. Keep me informed. I'm sorry, I really have to go now, Jayden is screaming from his cot. Good luck." Jessie rings off.

She sits for a moment, staring at her phone and thinking things through. She needs to talk to Kacey and also to Louise. Louise can tell Scott about her concerns over Stacey. There has to be some way to sort this mess out.

Her mobile suddenly rings. Mark. At last. Her heart skips and she pushes the answer call button. "Hello?"

"Mel." Mark sounds frosty, not at all like the caring lover she kissed goodbye on Sunday. "You never told me you work for Scott. I just got off a phone call from him." He pauses and she can almost feel his anger rushing through the phone line at her. "Do you realize I had a lot riding on this submission, too? The fact you have shared the information with the opposition means I've lost a potentially lucrative contract. They'll go ahead and undercut all our prices and we'll lose the business."

"Wait. I didn't do anything. I did not send that email." Mel is desperate to make Mark understand.

Mark scoffs. "Well if it wasn't you, who did? Scott said you are the only one who has the information. He didn't give it to anyone else."

"I'm not arguing with you about this, Mark. You obviously don't believe me and that's your choice. Why didn't you answer my text?"

"What? Don't change the subject." Mark does not attempt to hide his annoyance.

She sighs, feeling as if the entire world is conspiring against her. "I really enjoyed the time I spent with you, Mark. I thought we had a connection. I'm sorry you've been caught up in this issue at work. I'm trying to sort it out, though of course I can't change the fact that our competitors now know what we are doing. I am going to work hard to clear my name."

"I've got to go. Goodbye, Mel." Mark hangs up without waiting for her reply.

She drops the phone, puts her head in her hands, and sobs. *How had her life turned itself upside down again so quickly?* She switches on the engine and drives home, wanting only to crawl into her bed and never emerge again.

She falls into an exhausted sleep. Tangled in the bedsheets, she has a headache and is nauseous. She wakes at three a.m., disoriented and chilled. She gets up from the bed, pulls the curtains closed, and steps over the pile of clothes she dropped in the middle of the floor. She pours herself a large glass of water and carries it back to bed. She sips at her drink and stares sightlessly at the bedroom wall. *She needs to clear her name, but how?*

Cherie Mitchell

She sleeps intermittently until seven a.m., and then lies awake in her bed, unable to stop shivering. There is no reason to get up. The wonderful job she loves is now gone, and it seems her budding relationship with Mark is also over before it began. He is not interested in her explanations and he gave her no reason for not calling or texting. She stays in bed most of the day, feeling headachy and dull. She does not have the energy to get up or any interest in getting dressed. She mopes around the house over the next two days, unable to concentrate on anything.

Finally, on Friday morning, she wakes up feeling a little more positive. She is resolved to clear her name and she is finally feeling strong enough to begin to fight.

9

Mel opens her laptop and types an email to Kacey, asking if Stacey was in the office on Monday whilst she and Scott were out dealing with the rental car. Next, she emails Louise, asking first if her daughter is well, and second, if she is willing to back her up if she tells Scott about Stacey poking around in the office while Louise was away sick. She pushes send on both emails, and then waits.

It is midmorning before she hears the ping of an arriving email and checks her laptop to find a message from Kacey. It is a short reply saying yes, Stacey was in the office while Scott and Mel were away on Monday, and that she is sorry Mel left company. There is no reply from Louise yet. She chews her thumb nail nervously. The biggest part of her plan is based upon Louise agreeing to help.

Louise finally replies, just after three. She says her daughter is well and she is sorry Mel has been let go. She also says she spoke to Scott about Stacey being in her office and he dismissed it as irrelevant to the issue. She ends the email saying she hopes Mel is coping okay and perhaps they can have coffee one day.

She stares at the email in dismay. *What can she do now?* She needs to talk to Scott and get him to listen to her, but he told her in no uncertain terms there is nothing further to discuss. There is no point in returning to the office to try and see him. She suddenly feels claustrophobic and trapped. She needs to go outside and fill her lungs with fresh air. She puts on her walking shoes and drives up the Port Hills to her beloved Victoria Park, her mind turning over with suggestions that she just as quickly discounts. *There has to be a way through this, but what is it?*

She starts off around the hill face on her favourite track. The wind is brisk and unforgiving, and perfect for clearing her head. She reaches the outcrop where she met Mark. Where Mark stumbled and twisted his ankle. It could have been the start of something wonderful, begun by something as simple as a stumble and a misstep. She stops suddenly. Of course, that is it.

She remembers the night she was rushing to meet Ben and she broke her heel as she stumbled through the door into the restaurant. Scott caught her as she fell, although she did not know him at that stage and he never made any indication he remembered her. The important thing is she knows from managing his Outlook calendar he has been back to the same bar and restaurant several times, for casual after-work drinks or dinners with clients. She knows she has no chance of speaking with him at the office, but perhaps she can find him at the restaurant and convince him to listen to her.

She checks the time. It is already after five, and today is Friday. *Perhaps Scott will be visiting the restaurant tonight?* She hurries to her car, her feet pounding on the dirt path. She drives home to quickly shower and change clothes. She makes it to the restaurant before six-thirty, perfect timing when hoping to catch someone having after-work drinks. She gazes around the bar, but there is no sign of him in the mass of business-suited men.

Not allowing herself to feel deflated, she orders a drink and carries it over to a vacant table to wait.

"How is your night going?"

She looks up to see a red-haired man standing beside her table, with a glass of beer in his hand and a look of open admiration on his face. "It's going fine, thanks." She turns away dismissively, hoping the man will get the point. She is in no mood to be picked up. She needs to have her wits about her in case Scott walks in the door.

"Are you here by yourself? What's a good-looking girl like you doing all alone on a Friday night?" He looks smug now, as if he thinks he stands a good chance.

"I'm waiting for a friend, but there is no reason a woman can't have a drink on her own. You're on your own, aren't you?"

"No, I'm with my friends." He indicates vaguely across to the other side of the bar where a group of rowdy and loud men are standing. "Can I sit down?"

"I can't really stop you. But to be honest, I'm not in the mood to talk. As I said, I'm waiting for a friend."

The man sits down, anyway. "I'm Kevin."

"Hi. I'm Mel." She pulls out her phone and begins to study it, scrolling through her screens and ignoring the man. She darts another glance at the door as it opens, but there is still no sign of Scott.

"So, Mel, what do you do for a living?"

She sighs and puts her phone down on the table. He is not taking the hint and it is time to drop any subtlety. "Kevin, I'm sure you're a nice guy. But I've got a lot on my mind and I'm waiting for someone. I don't want to miss him if he comes in."

Kevin scowls at her. He is clearly not used to being given the brush off and his annoyance is apparent. He drains his glass and sits down on the table top. "Suit yourself," he said brusquely. "Uppity bitch."

She rolls her eyes and watches as he walks to a group of girls by the window. She shakes her head as he places a hand on one girl's bum, only to have it slapped away. She suppresses another sigh. It seems that good men are hard to find, and unfortunately she was wrong about Mark too. He only called her in the end because of the issue with the leaked email. She gazes glumly out the window and waits until the after-work crowd begins to thin out and she is sure Scott will not be coming, at least not tonight.

On Saturday morning, she gets out of bed early and goes for a long walk. She knows she needs to keep herself busy and stop thinking too much, shying away from dark thoughts about how her life has spiralled into a black hole. Slowly, the day passes and once again she prepares herself to go to the bar and wait for Scott.

She does her hair and applies makeup. She adds a triple layer of mascara and draws a dark line of kohl along her lower eyelid. She winds up her favourite tube of lipstick and carefully colours her lips. She chooses slim, black pants and a flattering red top. Checking her reflection in the mirror, she looks pretty and a little dangerous, which is exactly how she feels. Perfect.

She orders a drink at the bar and looks around for Scott. She finds a table and sits down to people-watch and wait. As she gazes around the groups of diners and drinkers, she suddenly notices Scott sitting at a booth with a couple of other men. Her pulse quickens. Her plan is under way – she just needs the chance to talk to him now.

She waits, biding her time. She knows she does not want to approach him while he is sitting with the others. She is relieved when he walks to the bar to order drinks and stands with his back to where she is seated at the table. She walks over and leans casually on the bar beside him, setting her empty glass down as if she just came up to order a drink. "Hi Scott," she murmurs.

He turns to her, a ready smile on his face, which immediately fades when he sees Mel. He nods curtly. "Mel."

She takes deep breath and hurries on. "Scott, I need to speak with you. I was unfairly dismissed and I did not have a chance to defend myself or even to speak. I would like to have that opportunity, please. Someone else sent that email and I think I know who it was."

Scott picks up his drinks from the bar. Ignoring her, he thanks the barman and turns back toward his friends. He begins walking away before he says, "Mel, this is not the time nor the place for this conversation."

"Wait." She puts her hand on his arm and looks at him, pleading. "Scott, please. Can you give me the chance to talk? If not here, can we meet somewhere else? Please?"

He sighs. "Alright. I can give you thirty minutes Monday morning. I will meet you at eight-thirty at the Blue Water for a coffee. I'm only doing this because I think you are a good person at heart. We can all learn from our mistakes." He walks back to his table, leaving her feeling relieved and hopeful that everything might have a chance to be put right after all.

"Hi."

She turns to face the man who is now leaning on the bar beside her, half expecting to see Kevin again. A balding guy in a cheap suit nods toward Scott's retreating back. "I can't believe that guy just walked off and left a beautiful woman standing here at the bar on her own. Can I get you a drink?" He leers at her before dropping his eyes to stare openly at her breasts.

She glares at him, and then glances down to where his left hand rests on the bar, complete with a wedding ring.

"I'll tell you what, let's phone your wife and invite her along as well. You can get us both drunk and then perhaps we can have a threesome." She tosses her head and marches out of the bar. She is obviously a hopeless case. There is something about her that attracts the wrong type of men.

Cherie Mitchell

Perhaps she is destined to be single unless she is willing to lower her standards. *She is not prepared to do that.*

She now has to speak with Louise and convince her to come with her to talk to Scott. She suddenly remembers her husband is keen on go-karts and the family spends most Sundays at the track. She feels another stirring of hope. Tomorrow she will go to the track and try to persuade Louise to do what is right.

Cherie Mitchell

10

Mel is ready early in the morning, fully prepared to do whatever it takes. She searches for the go-cart track online and checks the opening times. Arriving at the track not long after the ticket office opens, she finds a park and walks through the gates, searching the throngs of people for any sign of Louise's familiar face. Go-carts are a popular hobby, so a large crowd is already gathering. She begins thinking her search is hopeless when she walks around the front of the stands and there is Louise, crouching down beside a little girl in a stroller.

"Hello, Louise."

"Oh, Mel. What are you doing here?"

"I have to talk to you. Can we go and sit down?" She leans over and smiles at the small girl in the pushchair. "Hello Elisa. Aren't you the prettiest little thing? I need to talk to your mommy."

Louise hesitates, biting her lip. Finally, she nods and steers the stroller over to a row of empty seats. She scrabbles in her bag and finds a soft toy for Elisa. Elisa

Cherie Mitchell

sticks her thumb in her mouth and snuggled down with the teddy, her big eyes fixed on Mel's face.

She gets straight to the point. "Louise, I need you on my side with this. I want my job back. I love working there and I thought you and I were starting to form a good friendship."

Louise nods slowly. "We were. I like you. I am sorry about what happened."

"I managed to get in touch with Scott and he has agreed to meet with me briefly Monday morning at the Blue Water. Is there any chance you can stop by and put in a word for me? We both know Stacey framed me by sending the email from my computer."

Louise winds her wedding ring round and round her finger. "Yes Mel, I completely agree with you about Stacey, but she is my boss's girlfriend. I tried to speak with Scott already and he does not want to know. I don't like your chances of changing his mind, I really don't. If you do manage to convince him that Stacey sent the email, she will make your life at that company so miserable you will not want to stay anyway."

"I just need to clear my name. I can deal with Stacey after I've done that." She places her hand on Louise's arm. "Please?"

Louise hesitates before blowing out a long breath. "Ok. I will stop in at Blue Water tomorrow, but only for a few minutes."

"Thank you. I *have* to give this a shot. It's my only chance."

Louise looks up and smiles as a lanky sandy-haired man walks toward them. He bends to ruffle Elisa's hair and looks curiously at Mel. "Hi."

"Cam, this is Mel, the girl I was telling you about." Louise and Cameron exchange glances and Mel does not need to be a mind reader to guess what he is thinking. He thrusts out his hand, his expression solemn. "Pleased to meet you, Mel."

"Mel is meeting Scott tomorrow morning and I agreed to stop in and explain how Stacey has been snooping around everyone's desks."

Cameron frowns. "Be careful, love. You could get yourself into a lot of trouble by trying to drive a wedge between a man and his girlfriend. You need this job. You already know that."

Louise looks at Mel and gives her a brave smile. "We'll be fine. I want to help."

***

The next morning, Mel pulls on a soft and flowing white dress and applies a minimal amount of makeup. She fluffs her short hair around her head until it looks like a mini halo. She hopes she is conveying innocence. She needs to try every trick in the book. She is determined to convince Scott she is not responsible for sending the email and somehow get her job back.

She drives toward town, stopping first to pick up some paperwork to support the case she is about to put forward. She finds a parking space outside the café and orders a coffee. The waitress brings her coffee over just as Louise walks in the door, her nervousness apparent. "Thanks for coming, Louise. Scott hasn't arrived yet."

Louise twists a strand of hair anxiously between her slim fingers. "I'm not sure how he's going to take this."

The women have nearly finished their coffees when Scott finally arrives. He walks in the door and looks around, his face folding into a frown when he sees Louise sitting at the table with her. He walks over to join them, his expression dark. Mel swallows the lump in her throat.

"Mel." He nods at her before turning to Louise. "I'm surprised to see you here, Louise."

Louise sits up straight and tips her chin up. "I thought it was important for me to be here."

Scott looks at his watch and sighs. "I don't have long, ladies."

Mel takes a breath and rushes in. "I asked you to meet me and give me the chance to defend myself. I realize it is incriminating for the email to be sent from my own address, but I swear I did not send it. Someone framed me."

Louise nods. "I'm standing by what Mel says." Her voice wavers. "I also have to point out that Stacey has been in the office a lot lately while you have been off site. Mel caught her sitting in my office and looking at my computer when I was away sick last week."

"Stacey is my girlfriend and as such is privy to many of my activities." Scott makes no attempt to keep the annoyance from his voice. "I talk to her about my work and she always shows an interest. I expect she was just making sure there was nothing important that needed to be done in your absence. I'm not sure what you're trying to say, Louise, but I'm not sure I like it."

Louise glances at Mel. She looks terrified. Mel reaches under the table to give her knee a quick, reassuring squeeze.

Mel reaches into her briefcase and places the papers she collected before their meeting face down on the table in front of her. She smiles across the table at Louise. "Thank you for your support, Louise." She looks at Scott, determined to prove her innocence with the facts. "Can you remember the day your car broke down and you asked me to drop you off to pick up a rental car? The day the email was sent?"

Scott nods. "Of course, but I'm not sure what that has to do with anything."

Mel turns the papers on the table over and pushes them toward him. He looks at them and then looks back at Mel, frowning. "This is the rental car contract. Why are you showing me this? What has this got to do with the confidentiality issue?"

Mel taps her finger on some figures and a scrawled signature near the top of the front page. "Look at the time and date of the booking. This was when you collected the keys and signed the contract, just after I dropped you off. You've signed it."

Scott's frown deepens. "What is your point, Mel?"

"Please, go back to the office and check the time and date on the email that was sent from my computer. I can guarantee you will find it was sent around the same time as the car was collected. I was out of the office when the email was sent and this is proof."

Louise leans forward, her voice now strong and commanding. "Scott, can you please go and do that right now? You have accused Mel of something she did not do and now she has shown you proof. While you're at it, can you check with Kacey and see what time Stacey was in the office that day?"

A mixture of emotions flickers across Scott's face, an intriguing combination of guilt, sympathy, and frustration. He picks up the paperwork and quickly stands up. "Mel, if you are correct, I owe you an apology. I have to get to the bottom of this. I'm going back to the office now and I'll phone you shortly. Rest assured, if these times match up your job will be reinstated immediately, with two weeks full pay to compensate for the hours you lost last week. I'll call you as soon as possible."

The women watch Scott leave before Louise leans over the table and hugs Mel. "Wow, that was brilliant. How did you think of that?"

Mel smiles. "It was my visit to the go-kart track that gave me the idea. As I was leaving, I saw the hire go-karts lined up at by the gate for rent and a lightbulb went off in my head. I knew Scott must've signed a contract with the time and date the rental car hire began, and as soon as I got home I rung the company to check."

"Very clever." Louise pulls out her phone and checks the time. "I need to get to work. Promise you'll phone me as soon as you hear from Scott?"

Mel follows her friend out the door. "I'm going to walk alongside the river while I wait for his call. I'm too nervous to do anything else." She sets off along the riverbank, feeling on edge and anxious. *Surely, he can now see she is telling the truth?* She checks her phone, again. *What is happening? Why is he taking so long to call her?*

When her phone finally rings, she nearly jumps out of her skin. She fumbles to answer it, closing her eyes for just an instant and throwing a small prayer into the ether. "Hello?"

"Mel, please accept my deepest apologies. I am so sorry I didn't give you the chance to explain. The time printed on the rental car contract and the time on the email are only a few minutes apart. There is no way you could've been back at your desk in time to send the email. Once again, I'm so sorry. Are you willing to return to your job? To be honest, I'm half expecting you to tell me you're taking me to the employment courts and you're probably well within your rights to do so."

"No, I'm not going to the employment courts. I understand how incriminating the whole situation is. Generally, an email does come from the person it says it comes from. "She feels an enormous sense of relief, even though her legs feel as if they can scarcely support her. She falls onto a nearby park bench, glad of the support. Her name has been cleared. "I would love to come back, but on two conditions."

Cherie Mitchell

"What are they?" Scott asks, cautiously.

She hides a smile. She can imagine the dollar signs running through Scott's head. "First, I need you to tell Stacey she is not allowed in the back offices when you're out. Second, can I ask you to call Mark, the printer, and tell him I am innocent?"

"Mark? The printer?" His confusion is apparent.

"Yes, he's the man who owns the printing company which is listed on the leaked email. Can you please call him and tell him it was all an awful mistake?"

"I won't ask why, but yes, of course I can. And leave Stacey to me. Mel, when can you come back? I have so much work for you to do and to be honest I was devastated I had to let you go. You'll be paid for the days you were away, of course." He clears his throat. "Your professionalism throughout this entire mess has demonstrated to me, again, that you are a valuable employee and exactly the type of employee this company needs. I think we can also come to some kind of uh, monetary compensation."

"I can start back tomorrow, but I sincerely hope you'll give me the benefit of the doubt in the future."

"Of course." Scott thanks her, apologizes again, and tells her he will ring Mark right away.

Mel walks back to her car, feeling buoyant and relieved, but also a little sad. It is not a comfortable feeling to know Stacey attempted to sabotage her job and nearly succeeded. Mel has never had anyone hate her that much before, especially someone who barely knows her.

Her phone rings just as she inserts the key in the ignition. Mark. She picks up without hesitation.

"Mel, Scott just called me. I am so relieved. I didn't want to believe you could do such a thing, and I shouldn't have doubted you in the first place. I'm so sorry. My instincts said this was not something you would do. I should've listened to my gut. I've been thinking of you constantly over the last few days and I already made up my mind to call you later in the week and check on you. Mel, when can I see you?"

"How about lunch today? I'll meet you at the Stag's Head, and it's your shout."

11

Mark looks more than a little shame-faced as he walks into the restaurant. Mel is already seated at a table. She watches as he pulls out a chair and sits down.

"Mel." He looks at her directly, his expression contrite and apologetic. "Again, I'm so sorry."

"I'm not mad about how you reacted to the work issue. As I said to Scott, it certainly did look as though I was the person at fault, and I understand you have a lot riding on that contract." She gazes back into those appealing eyes, unable to stay annoyed at him. "Mark, why didn't you call or text me? I thought we had a connection, but then you treated me like nothing more than a one-night stand."

"I'm sorry. I should have taken a moment to text you. Yes, I agree we have a connection and I certainly never saw you as a one-night stand." His voice breaks a little. "Mel, on Sunday night Rastus was hit by a car."

She gasps and her stomach drops. She never expected this. "Oh no. I'm so sorry. Is he...is he ok?"

Mark nods. "He'll be ok. He's still at the vet clinic. It was touch and go for the first few days and I was out of my mind with worry. That little dog means so much to me." He exhales. "I don't know what I'd do without him. My mind was so full of what was happening with him that I didn't think of texting you. Then Scott called and told me about what happened with the contract. It just felt as though everything caved in at once."

"I understand. I understand completely. I'm just glad Rastus is going to be ok." She meets his gaze again, hoping her eyes are conveying what she really wants to say. "I'm also glad I got the chance to see you again."

"Me too." His eyes twinkle at her. "Tell me more about what happened with the contract. I couldn't believe it when he mentioned Stacey has something to do with it."

She explains the story and tells him about Stacey's deceit. He listens, his brow creases, until she finishes. "Why would anyone do that to their partner? Did the silly girl not stop to think she was jeopardizing Scott's business in her attempt to get rid of you?"

"I'm not sure Stacey ever spends much time thinking. She is not the most aware person I've ever met."

The waitress arrives with the menus, and the couple turns their attention to lunch. Talk turns away from work and Stacey, and on to more interesting topics. Soon Mark looks regretfully at his watch. "I have to go. I have a meeting. Can I see you tomorrow tonight?"

"I'd love to see you tomorrow night."

Mark goes to the desk to the pay the bill and she smiles to herself. Everything is working out, even better than she hoped. At the door of the restaurant, he hugs and kisses her gently. "I promise I'll text." He gives her a wicked grin.

She laughs and kisses him back before heading to her car. Everything is perfect now, except for Stacey. Working at a company where the boss's envious and dangerous girlfriend has access to many of the day-to-day business transactions is a sure recipe for disaster. She will have to tread carefully.

She rings Jessie as soon as she gets home. "Jess. So much has happened. Do you have time to talk?" Jessie listens quietly as she explains everything. She tells Jessie how she has her job back and how she and Mark talked everything through.

Jessie tells her she is pleased, but she is very dubious about Mel returning to a work place where her boss did not trust her word over the word of his girlfriend. "Stacey will be even worse now, Mel. You know this."

She sighs. "I know. I'm worried about that, too."

As she hangs up, her mobile buzzes again. She glances at the screen and grins when she sees the message is from Mark. *I'm looking forward to tomorrow night.* She replies with a happy face. Everything will be fine. She just has to believe this.

***

When Mel walks into the reception the next morning, Kacey looks up, greets her warmly, and welcomes her back. To her surprise, Tim and Jack both come out of their offices and greet her enthusiastically, despite the fact she has not had much to do with them. Louise bounds out of her office and throws her arms around her. "Welcome back.

I'm so pleased you're here. I've got no doubt Scott has a ton of work for you, but will you meet me for lunch?"

She laughs and heads over to her desk. Scott's door is open. He looks up and beckons her in, asking her to shut the door behind her.

She sits down, remembering their last awful meeting in this office. Scott obviously notices her expression. "There is no need to be nervous, Mel. Once again, thank you for returning to work and I cannot apologize enough for the incident. I want to reassure you I will not doubt you again. Your work is efficient and prompt, and your personality is an asset to the office. I should never have doubted you in the first place." He clears his throat and looks down, fiddling with a pen on his desk before returning his gaze to her. "Mel, I don't generally discuss my private life in the office, but I feel you deserve to know this. Stacey and I have ended our relationship. She will not be back in the office again. That is all I want to say on the subject." He picks up some papers and hands them to her, resuming his normal professional persona. "Can I ask you to start on these? We have a meeting at ten and I'd like to view the agenda prior to the meeting. Also, can you book me a return trip to the

Auckland plant on Thursday?" He turns back to his computer.

She walks out of his office and pulls the door closed behind her. She really wants to dance with happiness after hearing Stacey will no longer be a thorn in her side. As she sits down, her phone pings with a text and she glances at the screen. It is Mark. "Good morning, beautiful. Thinking of you. C u 2nite."

Grinning, she puts her phone away and reaches over to switch on her computer. Yes, today is going to be a very good day, and somehow she knows it will be the start of many more.

The End